This Little Tiger book belongs to:

For Fred and his daddy, who always
find friends wherever they go ~ G D

For Phil and Jasper. Life is always
lovely when they come along too.
With love ~ C J-I

LITTLE TIGER PRESS LTD,
an imprint of the Little Tiger Group
1 Coda Studios, 189 Munster Road, London SW6 6AW
Imported into the EEA by Penguin Random House Ireland,
Morrison Chambers, 32 Nassau Street, Dublin D02 YH68
www.littletiger.co.uk

First published in Great Britain 2020
This edition published 2021

Text by Georgiana Deutsch
Text copyright © Little Tiger Press Ltd 2020
Illustrations copyright © Cally Johnson-Isaacs 2020
Cally Johnson-Isaacs has asserted her right to be identified as the illustrator
of this work under the Copyright, Designs and Patents Act, 1988
A CIP catalogue record for this book is available from the British Library

2 4 6 8 10 9 7 5 3

# Along Came A Fox

Georgiana Deutsch

Cally Johnson-Isaacs

LITTLE TIGER

LONDON

It was just the right sort of night
for finding fireflies, and Bramble was ready.

Silvery moon? Yep.

Sparkly stars? So many!

Unfortunately, Bramble didn't have
a clue where fireflies hide.

In that scratchy bush?
Nope.

How about under this cosy log?

"EEEK!" squeaked Hazel.
"You bounced me awake!"

"Sorry!" whispered Bramble, not very quietly. "I'm looking for fireflies!"

"Try the lake," hooted Twig, who knew **everything**.

"And wait for me!" Hazel called. "I want to see fireflies, too!"

Bramble scrambled down the misty,
twisty path. Hazel tiptoed behind,
through the creepy, crooked shadows.
"Spooky!" she shivered.

"Hurry up!" laughed Bramble.
Because foxes don't
get scared . . .

. . . do they?

"YIKES! A FOX!
WATCH OUT!" cried
Bramble, as she tumbled
head-over-tail and landed
SPLAT! on her bottom.

Poor Bramble.
How embarrassing!

"That fox made me jump!" grumped Bramble. She stomped back to the water and growled, "You're a VERY RUDE FOX!"

"You're a VERY RUDE FOX!
RUDE FOX! RUDE FOX!" came
the echoey reply.
"I'M rude?!" spluttered Bramble.
"I think you'll find it was YOU
who was rude!"

Hazel squeezed her eyes shut.
It was all getting a bit shouty.

Bramble bristled her whiskers.
"There's no room for rude foxes
in this forest!" she barked.
"Why don't you GO AWAY!"

"GO AWAY! GO AWAY! GO AWAY!" the other fox cried.

"That's IT!" snapped Bramble,
her nose in the air. "I'm
going to tell Twig!"

And with that, she stormed back
into the forest, with Hazel
hurrying after her.

Bramble told Twig everything.
Twig listened and nodded in
all the right places.

But then Twig said something very unexpected.
"I wonder what made that fox so angry?
Something must have upset him. Let's go
back to the lake together and ask him."

"I'm sure it wasn't so dark last time!" shivered Hazel.
"The moon is hiding behind the clouds," Twig explained.
She really did know everything.

Bramble was very quiet. "I got cross first,"
she whispered to herself. "Maybe that's what
made the other fox angry."

The lake was still. Bramble edged closer.
But when she peered into the water, she saw . . .

. . . NOTHING!

"The fox has VANISHED!" Bramble
cried sadly. "I wanted to make friends,
and now it's too late!"

Hazel couldn't bear to see Bramble upset.
She gave her a prickly hug. "Don't be sad.
We might still see some fireflies!"

But as the moon peeped out from behind the
clouds, they saw something EVEN BETTER . . .

"THE FOX IS BACK!" Bramble beamed.
"And he's SMILING, TOO!"
    Hazel laughed. "He brought FRIENDS!"
she squeaked, waving wildly.

"It just goes to show," nodded Twig, "that what we give out is what we get back. Tonight you gave that fox your smile, and that's exactly how friendships begin."

Bramble knew Twig was right. As usual.
"FOX!" she cried, bouncing in the air.
"LET'S BE FRIENDS!"

"LET'S BE FRIENDS!" laughed the other fox. "LET'S BE FRIENDS! LET'S BE FRIENDS!"

It was the perfect night for finding all sorts of things . . .

New friends? Three!
Fluttering fireflies? Too many to count!